Thomas
the Tank Engine

Based on *The Railway Series* by the Rev. W. Awdry
Illustrations by *Robin Davies and Jerry Smith*

EGMONT

EGMONT

We bring stories to life

This edition first published in Great Britain in 2012
by Egmont UK Limited
The Yellow Building, 1 Nicholas Road,
London W11 4AN

Thomas the Tank Engine & Friends™

CREATED BY BRITT ALLCROFT

Based on the Railway Series by the Reverend W Awdry
© 2012 Gullane (Thomas) LLC. A HIT Entertainment company.
Thomas the Tank Engine & Friends and Thomas & Friends are trademarks of Gullane (Thomas) Limited.
Thomas the Tank Engine & Friends and Design is Reg. U.S. Pat. & Tm. Off.

HiT entertainment

ISBN 978 0 6035 6832 9
55618/1
Printed in Italy

TO THE TRAINS ➜

This is a story about Thomas the Tank Engine. Thomas worked really hard, shunting coaches for the big engines. But what he wanted more than anything was his very own branch line ...

Thomas the Tank Engine had six small wheels, a short stumpy funnel, a short stumpy boiler and a short stumpy dome. He was a fussy little engine, always pulling coaches about. He pulled them to the station ready for the big engines to take out on journeys; and when trains came in, he pulled the empty coaches away so that the big engines could have a rest.

But what Thomas really wanted was his very own branch line. That way he would be a Really Useful Engine.

Thomas was a cheeky little engine. He thought no engine worked as hard as he did, and he liked playing tricks on the others.

One day, Gordon had just returned from pulling the big Express. He was very tired, and had just gone to sleep when Thomas came up beside him:

"WAKE UP, LAZYBONES!" whistled Thomas. "Do some hard work for a change!" And he ran off, laughing.

Gordon got a terrible shock. He decided he had to pay Thomas back.

The next morning, Thomas wouldn't wake up. His Driver and Fireman couldn't make him start. It was nearly time for Gordon's Express to leave. Gordon was waiting, but Thomas hadn't got his coaches ready.

At last Thomas started. "Oh dear! Oh dear!" he yawned.

"Poop! Poop! Poop! Hurry up, you!" said Gordon crossly.

"Peep! Peep! Peep! Hurry up yourself!" replied Thomas, cheekily.

Thomas usually pushed behind Gordon's train to help him start. But he was always uncoupled first, so that when the train was running nicely Thomas could stop and go back.

That morning, Gordon saw the perfect chance to pay Thomas back for giving him a fright. He started so quickly that the Guards forgot to uncouple Thomas.

Gordon moved slowly out of the station, pulling the train and Thomas with him. Then he started to go faster and faster – much too fast for Thomas!

"Peep! Peep! Stop! Stop!" whistled Thomas.

"Hurry, hurry, hurry, hurry!" laughed Gordon in front.

"You can't get away. You can't get away," giggled the coaches.

Poor Thomas was going faster than he had ever gone before. "I shall never be the same again," he thought, sadly. "My wheels will be quite worn out."

At last they stopped at a station. Thomas was uncoupled and given a long, long drink.

"Well, little Thomas," chuckled Gordon. "Now you know what hard work, means, don't you?"

Poor Thomas was too breathless to answer.

The next day, Thomas was working in the Yard. On a siding by themselves were some strange looking trucks.

"That's the breakdown train," said his Driver. "When there's an accident, the workmen use it to help clear and mend the line."

Just then, James came whistling through the Yard crying, "Help! Help!" His brake blocks were on fire and his trucks were pushing him faster and faster.

James disappeared into the distance.

Soon after, a bell rang in the signal box and a man came running.

"James is off the line! We need the breakdown train – quickly!" he shouted.

Thomas was coupled on to the breakdown train, and off he went as fast as he could.

"Bother those trucks and their tricks!" he said. "I hope James isn't hurt."

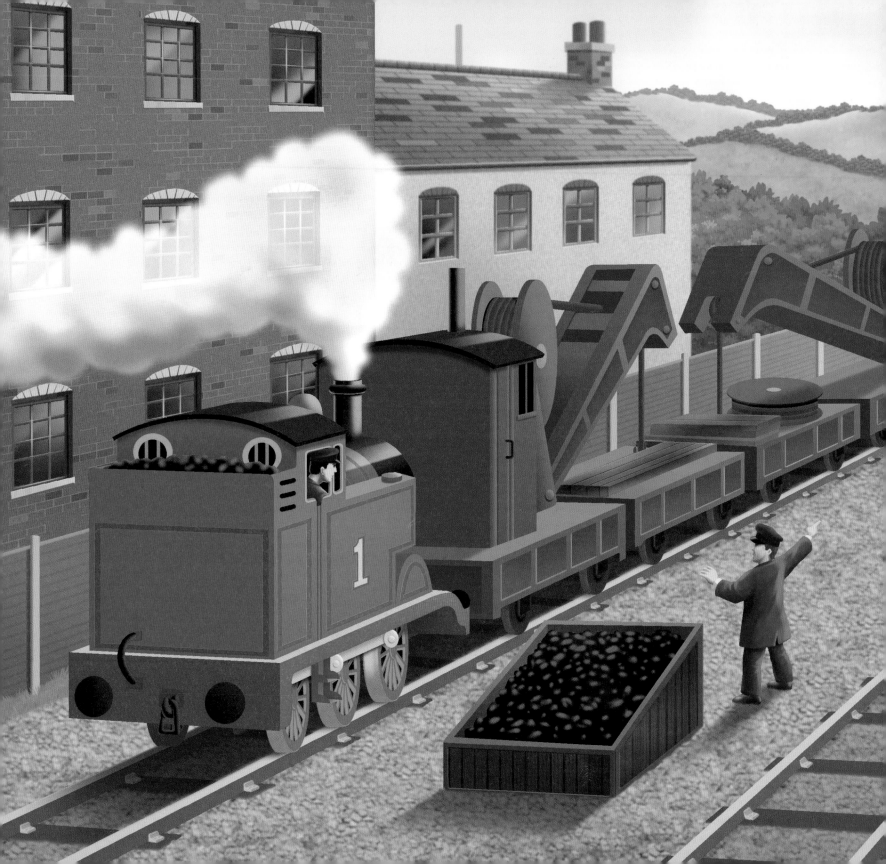

They found James and the trucks at a bend in the line. James was in a field, with a cow staring at him. The brake van and the last few trucks were still on the rails, but the front ones were piled in a heap behind James.

James' Driver and Fireman were checking to see if he was hurt. "Don't worry, James," his Driver said. "It wasn't your fault – it was those Troublesome Trucks."

Thomas pushed the breakdown train alongside James, then he pulled the trucks that were still on the line out of the way.

"Oh . . . dear! Oh . . . dear!" they groaned.

"Serves you right. Serves you right," puffed Thomas, crossly.

As soon as the other trucks were back on the line, Thomas pulled them away, too. He was hard at work all afternoon.

Using two cranes, the men put James carefully back on the rails. He tried to move, but he couldn't, so Thomas pulled him back to the shed.

The Fat Controller was waiting for them there.

"Well, Thomas," he said kindly, "I've heard all about it and I think you're a Really Useful Engine. I'm so pleased with you, that I'm going to give you your own branch line."

"Oh, thank you, Sir!" said Thomas, happily.

Now Thomas is as content as can be. He has a branch line all to himself, and he puffs proudly backwards and forwards from morning till night, with his coaches Annie and Clarabel.

Edward and Henry stop quite often at the junction to talk to him.

Gordon is always in a hurry and does not stop, but he never forgets to say, "Poop! Poop! Poop!" to Thomas; and Thomas always whistles, "Peep! Peep! Peep!" in return.